Kissin Kuzins

Forbidden Desires Unleashed

by H.G. Arthur, speaker and mentor

Dorrance Publishing Co
585 Alpha Drive
Suite 103
Pittsburgh, PA 15238
Visit our website at *www.dorrancebookstore.com*

ISBN: 979-8-88729-095-9
EISBN: 979-8-88729-595-4

Kissin Kuzins

Forbidden Desires Unleashed

It's amazing how we go through life reaping havoc on ourselves because growing up you sometimes don't understand what you're worth, or the things that happen to you, oh! but God knows. It's so amazing how when I look back at my past, I wonder did Jehovah ever love me for the things I did to myself and allowed others to do to me. How and why did He allow me to survive it all and live to tell it? Jehovah turned my life completely around and didn't hold anything against me, I mean, saved me from death, disease, rape, molestation, a dangerous love affair that could have and would have ruined a lot of lives…and so many other things, that would have taken me away from here! I know now that even if no one else heard my cry for help, I know that Jehovah heard me. This is my story and I hope it inspires many others to tell theirs.

I would like to dedicate this book to all the young women and men who embraced pain through the abuse and molestation from a family member or family friend, whom they trusted. Please know you have a voice and you have to speak up. Someone out there is listening. You just have to speak louder! In many homes, forbidden relationships are going on within families. We overlook this behavior because of shame and lack of respect for ourselves and our kids. It is time to wake up and pay attention to what's going on with our kids in our homes in the room next to us.

CHAPTER I
The Beginning of It All

I grew up in a small town called Stirling. If you have never heard of Stirling, it is a small town in Scotland. I was the youngest child of six children, four boys and my oldest sister. Now, we didn't have much, but the one thing my mom and my older sister and brothers made sure of, was that I felt loved. I overlooked the fact that we didn't have a lot of money, because it never felt that way to me. Now, for as long as I could remember, my mother was a woman who loved the Lord Jehovah and made sure we knew Jehovah too. No matter what happened in our lives, Mom would always tell us to pray about it; sometimes it helped, and sometimes I didn't think God was listening to me, depending on what I was praying about.

My father wasn't so much as into anything. I mean he was in my life but wasn't in my life, and I knew him, but I didn't know him as my father until one day I was walking to school and he stopped me and asked me if I knew who he was. I told him I had seen him talking to my mom, and that was all I knew. It did not matter because my older sister and brothers sometimes played the father role in my life. My sister was smart and was always taking charge of things when my mom wasn't around, and she did not take any mess from anyone. Now I can't tell you I remember a lot about my childhood, and some things are still a little cloudy in my mind, but one thing is for sure, I never will forget the first time I felt a penis press against my tiny little body. I think I was about eleven when it all began—the night I was introduced to my first forbidden love affair. And the funny thing is I was not afraid, because I just thought that this was the way my uncle Ace expressed how much he loved me other than buying me nice things.

CHAPTER II
Nice Things Come With a Price

It all started one Friday night. I spent the night with my cousins Anna and Asia; they are twin sisters. So that night we had made a camp in their living room with sheets and blankets, and we just ate and watched movies until we all fell asleep. My uncle Ace came in and woke me and told me he had something for me and asked me to come to the basement with him, and of course, I went because, like I said, he always gave me nice things. He asked me to sit on the bed and I did with excitement waiting to see my surprise and he gave me the most beautiful bracelet I have ever seen, and me being so excited I wanted to go wake my cousins, but he stopped me and told me that I had to give him a kiss to thank him, so I kissed him, but this kiss was different because it was longer and he had stuck his tongue in my mouth and laid me across the bed and laid on top of me and began to move up and down and I became afraid, but it was like I couldn't say anything.

He then pulled my little panties to the side and pressed his hard penis against my little vagina, breaking the skin to my small virgin vagina opening and when I say that was the worst feeling I had ever felt, but somehow I fell in love with it. I had begun to feel something I had never felt before as a teenager (butterflies in my soul) it lasted for a while and then he made this sighing sound and got up from me holding his hard penis as he wiped it with a towel next to the bed. I laid there in pain for a while and then I got up and began to walk towards the restroom that was in the basement to clean my slightly bleeding vagina. He then looked at me and said "Ladybug"—because that is what he called me—"now don't you say anything about this to anyone, especially not your cousins or your Aunt Dee because they wouldn't understand and your Aunt Dee would hate the both of us and you wouldn't be able to see the twins anymore."

He also said that we both will go to jail and it would be dangerous for the both of us. I nodded OK and went to the restroom and then back to the living room where the twins were lying sleeping still. The next morning when I got up, my uncle walked past and winked his eye and smiled at me. Later that morning, his wife asked where did I get the bracelet because she didn't see it last night and I told her it was from my friend at school, that it was in my bag. But the way she looked at me was as if she knew that wasn't the truth. But I had promised I wouldn't say anything. I guess you can say that I was afraid of the danger my uncle had told me about.

FORBIDDEN AND TRUE!

Hello, my beautiful niece, I have something nice for you. You must keep it a secret or the world will hate you, you can't say a word and do not tell a soul, because everyone will curse us both to the darkest of holes. I am sick in my

head I know that this is truth. I can't control my thoughts when I'm around you. This thing that I have done so awful and so true, but in a perfect world it would be forbidden too!

CHAPTER III
Embracing Pain and Loving Danger!

How I felt this was so right! June 1986 school is out and we now live in our new home in the city. It's about twenty-five miles from my cousins' house, but there was a candy store and a grocery store right in the neighborhood not far from where we moved. I had begun to make new friends and I didn't see my uncle Ace or my cousins that much anymore and it was OK cause I still got the chance to see my cousins when they came in the city. I had begun to come into my own by this time, (you know I started feeling myself). I had met these two girls and their names were Pat and Tara and this guy named Alex, and we all became good friends. There was also a barbershop called Nexted Up and a candy store on the next block called Belvedere, where Pat and Alex lived. I started going into the barbershop with one of my brothers and I would go to the candy store on my way to school with Pat and Alex. I especially liked the candy store because whenever I would go into the store, the owner would always give me these big chocolate balls and I would eat them like there was no tomorrow (laughing loudly) and that is how I got the name "chocolate drop." Yes because I loved the chocolate balls but also because I was a gorgeous dark-skinned child that lit up a room!

Two months out of school, my summer was going great until danger appeared. During that summer, my cousins from Croy came to visit. That's about 11.8 miles from where I lived in Stirling. It would have been my first time meeting them, but I was alright with that, until…! My cousin Linnell came in with my brother Deon, and I was sitting on the couch and he looked at me and asked my Deon who was I and my Deon said, "That's your cousin Cheri." I was pretty close to all my cousins, but when I saw Linnell, I felt a connection, I mean a different closeness. So, Deon introduced us and from that day on, he was my new favorite male cousin that I loved being around.

One day I was at my older sister's house and I was babysitting, Linnell had stopped by to see if my brother Deon was there and I told him that he wasn't there. He then asked me, "What are you doing?" and I answered, "Nothing. Just about to watch this movie." And he decided that he would wait for Deon and watch the movie with me. I kinda felt weird because this was my first time being alone with him and I was pretty nervous, but hey this was my cousin, so I didn't think anything crazy was going to happen, but then that day became somewhat like a replay of being at Uncle Ace's house. He asked me to come closer to him and I did and he began to rub my tiny little thighs and started kissing me. The whole time in my head, I was thinking this is just the way he shows he really loves me. After a few minutes, he laid me down on the couch and began sliding his nicely built body up and down my tiny body.

He then took his fingers and began caressing my vagina in and out, and at that point the feeling had taken over me, but there was no pain just a feeling that I have never experienced before not even with my uncle. Suddenly I just wasn't there anymore. I felt as if I had floated away; then there was a loud knock on the door and we both jumped up and I ran in the kitchen as if nothing ever happened and Deon walked in and asked Linnell how long had he been there and he told him he had just not too long got there before him and they walked out the door and began towards the game room, but then Linnell turned and came back and looked at me with a look that sent chills down my spine, and said, "See you tomorrow," and all I could do was just stare.

Now, I guess you can say I was really good at keeping things to myself, because I never mentioned what happened to anyone. One Saturday after that had happed My family was at this park having a family reunion and all of my cousins wanted to go swimming at the inside pool, and of course, I couldn't swim and everyone was in the deeper part of the pool and I was dying to get in and go down there with them, and my cousin Linnell yelled, "Hey come on in here!" So I had gotten in at the not-so-deep part. Linnell then yelled, "Come down here with us!" And of course I had gotten out of the part that I was in and went to the edge of the pool where he was and had gotten in with him. He was holding me in his arms, and I really didn't think about what had happened between us a couple weeks beforehand. I didn't think nothing was wrong with the way he was holding me and I was holding on to him. But then it happened he took his fingers and slid them in the side of my swimsuit and began to caress my vagina, once again. First, I didn't know what to do because we were in the deep end of the water and I was afraid to let him go because I couldn't swim, but the more I held on the more he caressed and that butterfly feeling came back in my stomach and this time it felt so good (I mean good).

Now, at the pool whenever they blew the whistle everyone had to get out of the pool, but he was still caressing my vagina and I was sinking into this wonderful feeling and the whistle blew and it was over. But the way he looked at me—as if I now belonged to him—is what made me realize I needed to stay away from him. Well, the whistle blew for us to get back in the pool and I simply decided that I was not going back in there although everyone was yelling for me to get back in at this point. I was too afraid, so I stayed out until it was time for us to leave. After the reunion, everyone went back to my auntie's house and the grown-ups sat in the house and did grown-up stuff and we played in the garage until it was time to leave.

That was the day that I invited a true sin in my life that was not so good for me! For the next two weeks, I didn't see my cousins because I had gotten on punishment for not being in the house on time. Back then we had to be in before the streetlights came on. I was a little hard-headed child that was curious about everything. The third weekend I had spent the night at my aunt's with all of my cousins, and Linnell was also there. We were sleeping in the guest room and Linnell was lying on the floor watching TV. I had gotten up to go to the bathroom in the middle of the night, and as I was getting back into bed, he pulled me down to the floor and began kissing me so passionately and I kissed him back. He began to caress my ass and my breast, and then it happened. He was pressing his penis, trying to get into my vagina and suddenly he was inside my vagina and he was hard as a country stone, but the strokes of his hard penis began to feel so good to me and the butterflies were just all over my body like never before and I fell in love with the pain, the pleasure and, yes, my cousin, my blood.

I did not know it was wrong to love him that way; it felt so right. Then we heard footsteps and we both stopped and I got into bed and pretended to be asleep. The next morning, we were all sitting at the table eating breakfast and Linnell just glared at me with this weird smile on his face. I think for the first time, I was starting to fill afraid and wanted to tell someone what had happened. I think then I felt like I was in over my head. I realize that this was, the exact thing that I had already went through with uncle Ace, a forbidden love for someone who had the very same blood as me flowing through his veins, and every time he looked at me my blood boiled like water in a pot. Here I was with secrets of blood relatives that only myself, Uncle Ace, and now Linnell and I shared except this one was different. It was one that I wanted to have forever. I guess I was getting good at keeping secrets whether they were meant to be or not even as forbidden as these were.

As time went on, we began to see each other all the time., I mean, because we all hung in the same areas and were always doing things together. But it became a little hard because every time we looked at each other, I knew I wanted to feel him inside me as much as he wanted to be. Although it was insane, I embraced it and to saw Linnell getting jealous because I had begun to invite other males into my life. Well, that made me feel very special and loved. Regardless we stroked each other every chance we got, not knowing whether or not someone was going to find out the forbidden passion we had for each other.

FORBIDDEN BLOOD!

The feel of his hands as he caressed my body, the softness of his lips as he kissed me so gently, his love flows within me forever with ecstasy, My **FORBIDDEN BLOOD** slowly he undresses me as I quiver with a speed of fear, firmly kissing me as he whispers in my ear, relax be calm as he grasps me in his arms My **FORBIDDEN BLOOD.** This love we shared was wrong from the start, but the danger I embraced of loving him I hid inside my heart, I pray one day I could lose this love, attachment from this **FORBIDDEN BLOOD.**

CHAPTER IV
Too Far In

September 1986 the summer was over and it was back to school and my cousins had left to go back to Croy. I felt that everything would go back to normal and I would forget all about my forbidden affair. I started seeing other guys and even had an affair with a female. I guess I was looking for a good love to replace a bad love. But little did I know that wonderful summer was just the start of a lifetime of nightmares for me. Linnell and his mother, grandmother, and two sisters had decided to move down to Stirling. Oh yeah, I was thinking the same thing, OH HELL NAWWW! this is not happening. It wasn't so bad at first because school was back in and I was hanging out with all my friends and I had felt like I was more mature and was able to make the right decisions for my life...so I thought!

There was this boy named Jeff. He and I had become really good friends and Jeff used to walk me home from school every day and we would sit out on the porch and talk about everything for hours. I mean he was a good person. No matter what, I could talk to him about anything I was feeling or thinking except my forbidden secret. One day it was nice out and Jeff and I decided to go get ice cream and we stopped by this nearby park to eat it. After eating the ice cream, we decided to just hang around out there. I mean, there were other people out there too and there were guys playing basketball on the court, and we were just talking and Jeff began to express how he felt about me.

I wasn't surprised because we spent a lot of time together. Then it happened—I kissed him. Out of all the months of our friendship, we had shared our very first kiss and it was so enduring and there we were right there fucking in the park, not caring that we were in a public park. I guess by now you're thinking I was pretty messed up. Well, I thought the same after so many years of figuring out that any man that showed me affection, I will give in to it. One weekend in 1987, Jeff and I went away together and everyone was looking for us, but we didn't care. We were together and looking forward to being with each other. We spent the whole weekend wrapping our bodies into each other. I mean, we explored each other like maps on a road trip, a trip that I enjoyed. By that time, I had gotten used to having sex, but he was so gentle and took his time with every inch of my body.

After the weekend was over, he dropped me off a block from my sister's house because that's where I lived at the time. We didn't see each other for a while after that. But to my surprise I'm at my sister's house and I get out of the shower and I'm in the bedroom getting dressed and Linnell walks in and tells me he really missed me. By that time I'm thinking about things a little clearer and I tell him that what happened with us was wrong and it had to stop. And this man looks at me and tells me it wasn't wrong and he couldn't stop seeing me and that he was really in love with me. What the hell! He grabbed me and began licking me all over. I mean, in spots that I never knew you could lick and it happened. We began fucking and I couldn't think about how right or wrong it was.

Yes, I was really messed up in the head, so messed up I started drinking like a sailor. I had even become rebellious for a while. By the time I started going to junior high school, and hanging out with the wrong crowd, skipping school, drinking, and smoking, coming in late, and dating older men, military men at that! I thought I was grown and could handle anything; I was fast but not a hoe fast. I guess you can say I was "looking for love in all the wrong places" fast. Trust me, I had my stipulations on who I wanted to have fun with. I had met this one guy that same summer named Eddie and he was handsome, but no matter who I was with, my forbidden lover would somehow run across my mind and I would think about his hands all over me and the stroke of his penis going in and out of me.

I guess I had begun to miss him and was looking for someone to fill that void. Yes, I was indeed screwed up a lot. I guess you can say I was mentally fucked up all around. I remember when I had met this guy name Derrick and he was military and fine too! Yes, too damn fine! We had gone out on a date if that's what you want to call it, and yes, we ended up fucking in his car, But the messed-up part is he had gonorrhea, and did not tell me he had gonorrhea. I had slept with another guy name Mark and that's how I found out I had it. Boy did that slow me down a bit! Well, I thought I was going to die. I was so embarrassed and scared. I mean, back then you didn't know the severity of the diseases that you had to concern yourself with, I only know that I had lain down with the wrong person that time and had paid for it.

At first, I didn't know what to do and didn't want to tell anyone, but I had to get help, so I told my best friend Pat, and we came up with the idea that I would tell my sister that I wanted to get on birth control, so she made me an appointment to the health department where I was treated, and yet again this was another problem and secret I had to keep to myself. I had gotten pretty good with keeping secrets, but this time I had a secret that I couldn't keep to myself not only did I have gonorrhea, but I had ended up pregnant, yes! You heard me correctly. I said pregnant! I thought to myself, *here I am not even finished high school and I am going to have a child*; I was scared and had no idea what I was going to do or how I was going to tell my mom or sister.

I felt like I had gotten pretty good at hiding things until one day I had skipped school to go to the clinic for a prenatal checkup and to see if I was cleared from the gonorrhea and had forgotten my wallet and the prenatal pills and they called my house to let me know and lo and behold my mother answers the phone and my brother was in his room, I heard my mom say to the caller, "You must be mistaken, because my daughter is only seventeen and she's not sleeping with boys." Yes, my heart fell and at that moment, I wanted to die. All I heard were footsteps coming down the hall and I never seen Jehovah God, but I was really wishing He would show up at that moment and save me from the death grip my mother had around my collar.

I thought at that moment that my mother was going to beat the life out of me, but she didn't. Yes, she was very upset and told me how I had disappointed her, but she accepted and I had no choice but to accept it because abortion was not an option. I mean, I had talked to the people at the clinic about adoption, but my mother stated that I was not going to do that either, she stated that I was going to finish school and raise that child. Of course, I thought, *who me?* Are you serious? This was not supposed to happen!

A MOTHER TO BE

What was I thinking, I'm only seventeen is this a nightmare? Wake me from this dream. I'm having a child. Is this really happening to me? I'm just a teen and a mother to be! Lord, please help me, please see me through because both this baby and I are really going to need you. Please my lord have mercy on me, I'm alone and scared at seventeen and a mother to be!

CHAPTER V
Demons, Demons, and More Demons!

I thought 1987 was going to be a good year for me. Being that I was pregnant, I thought that I could still enjoy life and be a teenager, but it didn't quite work that way. I was still hanging in the streets and drinking, smoking, having sex, and carrying on like somebody's fool. One morning I woke up to prepare for school and as I was taking my shower I begun to bleed, I mean blood gushing down my legs like a river flowing slowly. I started screaming like a crazy woman and my sister came in the bathroom and she started screaming like a mad woman, "Oh shit! Call the ambulance, Momma. This girl is dying!"

No, I was not dying I was having a miscarriage, but we didn't know that at the time. I guess that was the beginning of my depression and the mental thought that I just didn't care about anything anymore. I was out of school for a week and I had started drinking even heavier, hanging out more on school nights and just really acting the plum fool. Child I had even tried to smoke marijuana and that just didn't sit right with me, so I didn't try that anymore, I guess you can say I thought losing my child was a sign from God that I really didn't need a baby. I guess he heard my cry, so I thought! Again, I was young and stupid and did not know how God operated.

After having the miscarriage, I returned back to school and who is the first person I see but Linnell, and that wasn't good at all. I mean here I was trying to get away from my demons and this one walks right up to me and says, "I miss you. Can I see you after school?" like we are really dating, but of course you know seeing him was always my weakness, so I said yes and there I was right back in the arms of my forbidden blood, fucking like there was no tomorrow. This went on for the rest of the school year, but still no one knew our secret and as dark of a place as I was in, it could have went on forever because I found something along with the alcohol to help me cope with my mental state of mind after losing my child.

The end of 1987 was here and I wanted to try and make 1988 a better year. Of course I was still dealing with some things, but I thought that I could change a little. I had started working a job at a paper company being a secretary and I really enjoyed it. I would leave school go to meet Linnell and then go to work after we fucked most of the day. So Friday April 22 ,1988, I was about to leave work and my boss came to me and said that he needed me to come in on Saturday to help process some files and I agreed because he was my boss and it was my job. Well, later that day I was going to meet up with my girl Pat and we were going to this park called the circle. That is where everyone and their momma hung out at. I guess I felt that the more I hung out the more in control of my life I felt. Sounds crazy but that is what I felt.

Well, we stayed out at the circle till about 11:00 P.M. and then we went to this restaurant called Channels, which was another spot that everyone would go to and have breakfast or whatever. So while we were there, Linnell walks in and comes to the booth we were sitting in and sits right next to me and puts his hand between my legs, and yes it was very hard to contain myself as he caressed my vagina until it became so wet I had to make an excuse to go home by saying that I had to get up early for work. So Pat was like, "let's just order to go" and Linnell volunteered to take me home so that Pat wouldn't have to except we didn't go home. We went to a hotel and let me not forget we almost were seen by my other cousin Travis who was there with some older chick.

Saturday 23, 1988, I arrived at work at 9:00 A.M. and my boss was in his office, so I walked in to say good morning and he just stared at me while saying, "Good morning, you look beautiful this morning." And I just didn't know how to act. I mean, my boss was this fine, tall dark-haired, blue-eyed, "smell good all the time, looking like he had just stepped out of the *GQ Magazine* looking" guy. I smiled and said thank you because although fine as he was, his wife worked upstairs in the same building. I started to ask where were the files he wanted to process, but he stopped me and asked me to come and sit next to him and I did. He began to rub my shoulders and ask me if I liked my job and I said yes. Then he asked if I had a fella friend, and in my mind I wanted to say "yes, his name is Linnell," but I didn't. I said no; he then stated that I was such a beautiful young lady and he was shocked I didn't have a fella friend and began rubbing my breast, while kissing me. And it happened— next thing I know, he was licking me between my legs and then he slid his hard white penis in my vagina and we fucked for hours.

Afterwards he stated that the files could wait until Monday and I could just leave and go home and gave me $50.00 to take a taxi. I guess I didn't fill no type of way because he was my boss and out of all the ladies in the office, he chose me. HE was interested in me and that was all that mattered. I guess I was still looking for that type of love that was going to keep me full if that makes any kind of sense. You know you go through life doing things that you have gotten adapted to and to you it makes sense, but to others because they don't know you, they think that you are a maniac, not knowing that you are really mentally fucked up!

MENTALLY FROZEN!

I always go back to my first fuck, because in my mind it mentally fucked me up! My family, my blood, in my mind, my first love. I never knew the difference on why I was chosen. Did I bring this on myself without even knowing? Thinking will this be my life, a life that was chosen when I was just a little girl and now, I'm mentally frozen!

CHAPTER VI
My Life as a Wife and Mother

The year of 1988 and the summer is here and everyone is hanging out all over town. I mean, eastside, northside, and southside, up the hill, down the hill; I mean, everyone. Pat wanted to go out to the club Friday night, so I decided to stay at her house since her mom was going away and she would have the house to herself and we were planning to do everything we weren't supposed to be doing! (laughing). OK so Pat and I both went to work on Thursday but made up lies not to go to work on Friday so that we could start our weekend. Well, early Friday we decided to go to the liquor store to pick up our drinks for the weekend. Well, on our way back to her house, we ran into Linnell and his boy Courtney and they wanted to know why we wasn't at work, and of course, I told them none of their business and then they wanted to know what we were going to do later and we told them we were going to the club.

Now Pat nor Courtney had no idea that I was sleeping with my cousin and they were not about to find out either! Linnell looked at me as if his eyes were saying, *"I will see you later,"* and yes, mine said *"OKAY!"* with a big smile on my face, as I was walking away. When Pat and I got back to her house, we immediately started drinking, and while she fired up her joint, man, I can say we were taking shots after shots. Yeah, we were getting loaded. Lo and behold Linnell knocked at her door and pretended he needed me to ride with him to pick up his sister, and of course, that is not what we did. We went to a hotel room that he had gotten for the weekend and, yes, made love until we were tired.

OK my little rendezvous with Linnell was over and I was on my way back to Pat's house. Once I arrived to her house, I was getting out of the car and this fine-ass Puerto Rican guy name Javier walks up and asks me if I could tell him how to get to Libbie Avenue and, of course, I said, "Yes. Let me just let my girl know and I'll show you." Well, Pat decided to go with me because he was a stranger and she didn't trust him. As we all walked up the block to Libbie Avenue, he began to ask me my name and how old I was and Pat the same. I told him I was seventeen and then he asked if I was seeing someone and I wanted to say yes, but in reality it was no. So after walking a couple of blocks to Libbie Avenue, as he was thanking me, he asked if he could see me again and I said yes, and Pat and I turned to go back to her house. Pat and I had drunk so much, we were too tired and drunk to go out, so we just stayed in and watched movies until we fell asleep.

The next morning, we got up and both showered and got dressed and went to one of our favorite breakfast spots called Buds Breakfast Bar and ate breakfast before going on the block to see who was already out. People would come out pretty early and they would sleep with their doors opened because that was just how safe our town was. You could hang out all night, sleep with your door open and leave your car running as you go into the store. Speaking of the store—after Pat and I finished eating breakfast, we stopped by the store to pick up a couple of things for tonight and guess who I ran into. Javier and he was looking fine as hell with those basketball shorts and no shirt!! Whoo, child! I mean, both Pat and I had our tongues hanging out, but of course, I wanted him and I knew he wanted me.

Well, we started talking and then Pat saw this guy she was talking to and decided to go talk to him, leaving me and Javier alone. We talked and talked and he asked if I wanted to go across the street to the park, and there we were, right there in the park kissing each other like we had known each other forever. After that encounter Javier and I began seeing each other. We tried to see each other whenever we could and fucked every chance we got. We had gotten closer and closer together, and always somehow Linnell always managed to pull me into his world.

The summer was over and it was time to go back to school and there were just a few months before graduation. Little did I know my life was about to change, and at that time, it wasn't a good thing for me because Javier was an oiler and he was leaving to go back out on the water and I had gotten pregnant and was afraid to tell him, but thanks to Pat I did. After I told Javier I was pregnant, I ended up dropping out of school and we got married. After getting married, Javier and I moved away to Montana to start what I thought would be our new life together. Once in Montana I found out that I was pregnant and that is where my dream turned into a nightmare. I always kept in touch with Pat. I mean, because she was basically the only one who could talk me off the ledge when I felt like jumping and this was one of those times.

Surprisingly, when I finally decided to go to the doctor for prenatal care, I was already thirty-five weeks and scared as hell! Not because I was pregnant, but because I was alone. Here I thought that I had married the man of my dreams to find out I married a monster! I had this feeling, but I was just a woman without a cause, I was still carrying dark secrets that were buried deep inside that I wanted to let go of, but I just couldn't, for the life of me, let go. Once again, I started drinking, not even thinking about the child I was carrying. Wednesday night, December 21, 1989 and I felt like I wanted to pop, Javier came home and was so angry and I just didn't understand why, but then he screamed out, "Did you think I was stupid? Did you not think I wasn't going to question the fact that you were too far along for that child to belong to me?"

To be honest, I was stuck because I wasn't even sure myself. I mean, I had to question myself; like, did I really know? And that's when it happened. He hit me so hard the drink I was drinking dropped to the floor and blood, filled my mouth and I immediately fell to the floor. I guess it took him a minute to realize what he had done, before he reached down and picked me up while saying how sorry he was. Me I was kinda still in shock that it happened. Afterwards we talked and the next day, he made a decision that he didn't care whether or not the child was his, he claimed to love me and wanted us to be a family. Even with me still being unsure, but if he accepted the child, then I wasn't going to argue with him. I mean, I was afraid and felt as if I didn't have anyone but him. Yep, a woman without a cause or purpose, and I had to take what I could get. At that point I really felt kinda of low and had no control of my life, just like a woman without a cause.

WOMAN WITHOUT A CAUSE

I am a woman without a cause, trying to break free, holding on to my mistakes and dark memories. Lost in love, a broken lady, now I'm a wife and I'm having a baby. How can I carry out this task, behind the secrets and this mask, Lord oh! Lord, please help me before I lose it all. I'm bruised and broken, a woman without cause!

CHAPTER VII
Chained by Love, Baby, and Alcohol

Two years after I gave birth to my son, things started to get a little out of hand with me and Javier. He began staying out all night and I began to drink heavier and heavier. I had become depressed and lonely and I just felt as if I didn't care about anything anymore. I realized that I had to do something, because Javier had stopped going to work and I couldn't call my family, because I was a wife now and I felt like they wouldn't help me because I now had a husband. But there were two people I knew I could call on and that was my best friend Pat, and yes, the one person I tried to run away from Linnell! Like, how could I call this forbidden blood that I thought I had gotten away from. So, I called pat and she flew out to give me a hand. If I could have counted on anyone, it was Pat.

Once Pat arrived, I thought that things would be a lot easier, but boy was I wrong. Finally, I had gotten a job at this factory not too far from where we lived. I had to do something. Javier had just forgotten that he had a wife and a son. However, it was a Wednesday night and I was working and Pat was home with my son. There was this older lady that work with me and she use to sit and read the bible on her break. Well, this one night I was in a hurry to leave and I began to get sick. The old lady looked and me and said, "Child what's wrong with you?" and I stated that I had probably caught a bug, and she said, "Child that ain't know bug. Girl you're pregnant! "I thought to myself, *pregnant! Lady you got to be kidding me. I have one child now and I definitely don't need a second one.*

However, when I got home, I told Pat and she convinced me to go get a pregnancy test and just as the grass is green and the sun shines, I was carrying a second child! I didn't know how to tell Javier and didn't know how he would react given the situation, since he had just abandoned his family. But I was about to find that out, so I called him and asked if he could please come home because we needed to talk, and at first, he was hesitant but then said that he would be home in the morning. The next morning, I got up with no idea that beautiful morning was going to become my nightmare. Pat was in the kitchen making breakfast and my son was still sleeping. Pat looked at me with this crazy look on her face and I asked her what was wrong and she acted as if she couldn't get the words out of her mouth.

"Ladybug…." That's what she would call me sometimes. She said, "Javier won't be coming home, honey," and I ask her why? And she said that he was in jail.

"Jail!" I screamed. Why and how did she know this. Well, she had seen it on the news before I had gotten up. So I said, "Well let's go and get him!" Now despite everything he did to me, I still loved him and he was still my husband.

"Well, honey," she said, "we can't go there because we won't be able to see him."

"Why!" I'm shouting. "What happened?"

"He and another guy robbed a convenience store and the owner was killed." Right then I felt that I couldn't breathe and I was suffocating in my own thoughts that my life was over and what would I do alone with two kids. So, Friday, I got up after already being up all night crying and prayed to God: "Lord, if you hear me, please help me out, I really need you!" Like I said, I knew God I just didn't know how to use him! Help me, please! I think I was out of it that whole morning, but I looked at my son's face and it made me sink even deeper. Even though I had all this going on, I still had to feed my son. So I got dressed for work and kissed my son goodbye and went to work, while Pat watched my son. I just really felt so confused. That's the trick of the Satan to make you feel that way, to make you feel there's nothing left for you, and for a moment that's how I felt.

But Ms. Sanita the lady that was always reading the bible, was like my guardian angel. She knew something was wrong and was not going to allow me to work in the state of mind I was currently in, so she told me to go to the breakroom and she gave me some scriptures to go read and her bible. Now, I was against the idea and I knew how to read the bible, but I couldn't get no understanding from it. I mean, I was into church, but wasn't into church, if you can understand what that means. Anyway, I had already asked God to help me, so all I had to do is wait. That's what the old folks used to say, "Child, when you ask God for something you have to be patient and wait for him to answer you!"

I think…. Well, I had to put that aside and get to work. I had my son and a second baby on the way that I had to take care of. I don't know how, but I had to get it together. The following week, Javier had to go to court and Pat watched my son so that I could be there. I was not yet showing in my pregnancy, so he still didn't know. Of course, I fixed myself up. I mean, I couldn't let him see me looking a hot mess. When I arrived at the courthouse, I was met by his lawyer, who asked me if we owned any property and I politely said to him, "Sir, we don't even own ourselves let alone some property!" He then looked at me and said he was a public defender and stated that Javier may be going away for a long time, because without a good defense there was nothing he could really do for him except plead him out—whatever the hell that meant!

As we walked in the courtroom, Javier was sitting there looking so lost and sad, that I just wanted to cry out to the judge, "Let my man go!" But when they denied his bond, he looked at me as if to say *"this is it, we're over!"* and his life was over. He then looked at me and silently said he was sorry, (Yeah like that helped anything.) When they took him out his lawyer escorted me to go see him. Javier asked about his son and I told him he was fine and, with trembles in my voice, I added that his other child was fine too. He then said, "Are you kidding?" And I said no we have another child on the way.

At that moment, he seemed to be happy, but also in a sense of sadness. Either way I had to tell him and he needed to know what he had left me with. And a few minutes later, they took him away and I stayed for a while to gather my thoughts before leaving to go home.

LEFT TO LONELINESS

Dark days and silent nights, I'm left to loneliness and I have no fight! The man I love has gone away, left me to loneliness here I stay! Buried alive it hurt so deep, tossing and turning I cannot sleep. I need someone to hold me tight, to get me through this loneliness in this night!

CHAPTER VII
(Eleven Months Later) Moving in Loneliness

Today wasn't such a bad day, except Pat and I got into a disagreement about my drinking and smoking and not to mention I started hanging out with someone from my past that I thought would be my comfort, but ended up being my chaos! First, I started hanging out all night as if I wasn't carrying a child and second it seemed as if no matter what I did, nothing was going to fill that void of loneliness and affection that I thought I needed from Javier not being there. So finally I pushed the one person that I knew I could count on away. Yes, I had managed to push Pat away but not until I gave birth to another beautiful baby boy. She stayed for a couple of months, but the drinking and the partying continued and I had begun to sleep with random men to fill that void of loneliness once more. Now, here I was with two kids, no man, a part-time job, and no best friend because I had run her completely off. I mean, she will still call every now and then to see if I was still alive!

December the 7, 1992 was my birthday and I decided to spend it with my two favorite men—my sons. Well, I decided to run out to grab a couple stay-inside groceries. That's what Pat and I use to call it! While in the grocery store on the cereal aisle, I heard a familiar voice and my heart began pounding because I could not believe the voice I was hearing. So I made my way to the aisle next to me, and lo and behold in the flesh there he stood. Yes! Linnell the forbidden love of my life. At first, I tried to pretend that I didn't see but just his smell alone pulled me in! Child, before you know it, I stepped out and said with excitement "Hi, Linnell! Oh, my what are you doing here?" as if I really cared about that because just seeing him my vagina began to dance in my panties (whoo!)

He then looked at me and stated he had gotten engaged and moved here with his fiancée. In my mind I was saying, *you got to be kidding me* and then he stated, "You look really good. How are you?" and knowing I wanted to just say, *"I have two kids, my man is in prison, I'm working a part-time job that is barely getting me by, and I sleep with random men for comfort!"* But I kindly smiled and said, "I'm doing great! And I see you seem to be doing just fine." He said, "Yep, except I was missing you."

"Boy, go ahead. Don't do it, you're engaged!" So, after talking to him for about twenty minutes and he wanted to exchange numbers and we both walked away staring at each other in lust. Well, I left the store and arrived home and while taking the kids out of the car, lo and behold, my phone rang and you can only guess who it was. Yes! Linnell, and I answered with excitement but pretending not to be.

"Hey what's up, girl" is what he said, and me trying to refrain from the excitement stated, "Why I didn't expect you to call so soon." And he said, "I don't know why you would think that, girl. I miss that body and your kisses." In my mind I kept saying this is forbidden and I can't go back there, but he asked if he could come over, and I quickly answered yes, not even thinking about his fiancée. He then said, "Cool, what's the address? I'll be there in about an hour." So, once we hung up, I quickly got the kids inside, bathed, and fed them. It was about ten o'clock when he finally showed up with a cupcake with a lit candle on the top.

"Happy Birthday!" he said as he walked in the door.

"You remembered."

He said, "Girl, I remember everything about you, especially that sweet ass." And I was blushing from ear to ear. Like, how can something so forbidden feel so right! And of course, we sat and watched movies and caught up on things. Finally, my kids had fallen asleep and I put them to bed. After putting the kids to bed, we sat and talked and he talked about how he wanted to be there for me and the kids. Clearly, he saw my struggles, and then he leaned in and kissed me and I was no more. He slid his hand in my panties and began caressing my wet vagina, while sucking my breast until I just couldn't stand it anymore, so I un-zipped his pants and began caressing his penis until it was so hard that he had no choice but to slide it in my super wet vagina. And yep, right there on the floor, we began to make love like it was the very first time and I mean we didn't stop until we saw the break of day coming through the purple sheers hanging over the window.

Finally, about 7:30 the moment of not feeling lonely was over, and he had to leave to get home. Before leaving, he asked if he could come back tonight and I gladly invited him back, still taking no thought about his fiancée. I didn't care. God had answered my prayers, or so I thought. See, the enemy can dress things up to make you think your prayers were answered while it's just really his deceitful ass! That is why knowing the voice of God is so important, at least that's what my mom used to say. Well, while I was watching him leave dazed like a deer staring into headlights my alarm was going off for me to get the boys ready for daycare and get my shower and get to work. All day at work, I was in dreamland and could not wait to get off so that I could go back to that wonderful vacation of love and sex that I had endured the night before.

Five o' clock and it was time for me to leave work, pick up the boys, stop by the store, and get home to freshen up for another round of what I thought was heaven on earth! Boy was I in la la land. I mean, it was just the idea that I wasn't lonely anymore, even though what I was feeling was forbidden. So here we are again in bed screwing like two wild teenagers. Once we were done, I lay in his arms and we talked about him being there for me and my kids. Somehow, I was getting the idea that he thought one of them belonged to him. Go figure. Well, I guess he had forgotten that he was engaged, but I guess it did not matter, because we had been in love since we were kids.

As morning approached, he would get dressed, kiss me, and set a date for that night. So, this went on for months and then it turned into a year and his fiancée was no more and I began to feel trapped like he owned me. Of course, I was happy that he was there, but I began to feel afraid of what he felt for me, because he would always say, "You have always belonged to me." And that was his saying since the beginning of our forbidden relationship. March 17, 1997, Monday morning seemed like a normal day for me. I had gotten up like usual and gotten the kid's together, made coffee, and had gotten in the shower while the coffee was brewing. Linnell was still asleep, and like I said, it seemed like a normal Monday…until Linnell woke up.

He seemed to be in a good mood. He came into the bathroom and I thought he was going to greet me, but he began to ask why I was showering so early because I didn't have to work. And I before I could tell him I was going to drop the kids off and then run some errands, he slapped me so hard and blood filled my mouth and he just started arguing out of the blue, telling me I was going to see some other man and that if he found out who this other man was he was going to snatch the life out of me!" I guess you could say I was dazed from the slap, because it took me a minute to respond, I tried to ask him what was wrong and it didn't matter he was angry about something and he had already pegged me as the cause of his anger. He then began grabbing me and shaking me like somebody crazy!

I kept trying to get him to listen, but he just wasn't there. He threw me to the floor and began to rape me right there on the bathroom floor and for a minute I became numb and that man that I had loved making love to me was just a stranger inside of me. Once he was done, he wiped himself and left the bathroom, all I could do was just lie there and wonder what happened? And who was this man? After a few minutes of lying there, I got up and had gotten back in the shower to clean the blood from my mouth and wash all over again. After getting dressed and trying to cover the bruises with makeup I left the house to carry on with my day. I dropped the kids off at daycare and I just went and sat in the park to collect myself. About 1:00 P.M. I left the park and went and took care of some bills and then to get me some lunch, lo and behold I'm at this restaurant call Lenard's and Linnell walks in with two unfamiliar-looking guys that I've never seen before. Of course, I kept my distance. He had no idea I was there. I sat still in a corner until he left, then I got up and left just so that I could beat him home.

Luckily, I arrived home with the kids before he did so I made dinner, bathed the kids, fed them, and put them to bed. Linnell walked in about 8:00 P.M. and he acted as if nothing was ever wrong, and no I did not remind him of any of it. I could only pray that it would not happen again. About 10:00 P.M. he stepped in the basement to talk on the phone and I could hear him saying, "This bitch is getting on my nerves and if I didn't leave him alone, he was going to fuck me up!" Of course, I couldn't believe what I was hearing and all I could think of was what did I do. Like did he notice me at the restaurant and maybe thought I was spying on him? I don't know. I was just randomly coming up with what I could have done to make him angry at me.

He was in the basement for about two hours before finally coming back up the steps. I asked him was everything OK, and he just looked at me and said yes, as if I had said something wrong and I noticed that was becoming a pattern with us. I realized that there was no respect or loyalty between us like before. But I guess I should have expected that. I mean, I didn't have respect for myself at that time, so why should I have expected respect from him or any man (Ladies, that is called not loving and respecting yourself first.) So about 12:00 A.M. I said to him that, "I was going to bed and he didn't say anything at all. He just walked away. About 3:00 in the morning I could feel his long, hard penis sliding between my legs, and I tried to not give in, but I just couldn't hold back. I mean, after all, I loved fucking him plain and simple. I mean, I was so blinded and thought that this was how to love, not even thinking about it being forbidden.

After months I started to notice things were changing between us. We were arguing every day and he had begun to start beating me more and more as if I was his personal slave. He was always accusing me of other guys and he had even begun to camp across the street from my job and just say mean and hateful things to me. I had become the source of his anger and resentment and I don't know how this could have happened. It was a Tuesday night in 1998, Linnell had received a phone call, so of course, he goes to the basement to take it. I was just getting the boys settled down and I heard him shouting and screaming, and throwing things. I ran down to see what was wrong and he struck me across my head and began beating so badly.

I felt the blows but after a while I couldn't feel anything. He just kept saying, "It's you! It's all you! What are you doing to me? It's you!" was all he kept yelling and I couldn't think what I had done, and he just kept beating me until he was tired and finally, I couldn't feel, hear or see anything. I must have passed out, and when I woke, he had me in his arms screaming baby I'm sorry! I'm so sorry please forgive me! At that point I didn't what him to beat me again so I kept repeatedly saying, "It's OK, honey. I forgive you! (Boy was I stupid!) But again I was trapped in this crazy life I created with someone that had the same blood as me. The rest of the night, we made love, and afterwards he got up and went into the living room and I lay there deep in thought wondering what was happening to us, what was happening to me?

The next day after dropping the kids off, I went to work and ran into Ms. Sanita in the break room and she wanted to know was everything alright with me, and I told her yes, but I just really wanted to shout No PLEASE HELP ME! Then she looked at me and said, "I want to invite you to a revival on Saturday, I mean I wanted to say no, but it's like my mind was saying you need to be there. I accepted her offer and began to say I needed to find a sitter and she said no need, my niece will watch the boys and they could stay at her house, and she was going to pick me up, so I said sure OK. After leaving work when I arrived home, Linnell was asleep on the couch, so I quietly took the kids and left the house to take them to get some food, and upon returning, we just sat in the car before going back inside. Finally, I got up the nerve to go back inside and Linnell was sitting there watching TV and he looked up and asked where was I. I told him we went to get food. He started saying that I make him angry by the things I was doing. In my head, I was wondering what was it I was doing besides loving him!

I guess I had a price to pay and when I accepted him back in my life, I was paying it. He sat a few minutes and then left the house. I didn't see him anymore until the Friday before the revival. He stumbled in the house really drunk and high and just kept repeating "you try and leave I'm going to kill you." It was then I knew I had to get away. He finally fell asleep and I went to the bedroom with the kids and laid them in the bed next to me. The next morning, he came in the room and began to caress me while I was lying next to the kids as if they weren't even there. I didn't want to upset him, so I began to kiss and caress him back until we began to fuck right there, and it just didn't feel right. I felt like I was sinking into a hole and could not get out, once he was done, He got up and left the room not saying a thing. I immediately got up bathed and dressed the kids, and then I showered got dressed with what I was going to wear to the revival. About 5:30 P.M. I called Ms. Sanita and told her I was ready to be picked up.

MY ESCAPE

I'm walking into darkness and I hope it's not too late. Lord, show me the light for heaven's sake. Allow me to find you in this dark, dark hour. I'm weak and broken. I have no power! Save me, O Lord, I hope it's not too late, lift me from this Hell I'm in, please be my escape!

CHAPTER IX
The Night of the Revival

Ms. Sanita picked me up and we dropped the kids off at her house with her niece and left for the revival. Once we arrived, the building was packed with so many people and I kinda felt out of place. Ms. Sanita wanted to sit closer towards the front, but I was too afraid, so I sat near the back. People were greeting me and I was just so uncomfortable and I would speak and just sit there. The pastor began preaching and the more I sat and listened, I just began to cry a little, and then all of a sudden, He pointed at me and asked me to come to the front and I started looking around like he can't be talking to me. And the more I sat there, he just kept saying, "You" and pointing, "YEAH YOU!" he shouted. "COME HERE!" So I got up and began walking towards him, and as I got closer, I began to cry even harder as I stood in front of him.

He began to say, "God has heard your cry, daughter. After tonight, your whole life is going to change," and then he began praying for me and the more he prayed the more I cried until finally I fell to the floor and my body began to heat up as if I had this warm blanket covering me. I couldn't do anything. It was like

I was meant to lay there like a newborn baby. Afterwards I finally got up and he said, "Now go home and clean your house." Whatever that meant…I mean, I kept my house pretty clean. Then he said, "When you awake in the morning, I want you to read Psalms 23:35–38 in the bible over and over again." So, after we left the revival, Ms. Sanita said, "Leave the kids with me tonight and I will bring them home tomorrow." So I did as she said. She dropped me off at home and I went inside and the house was pitch dark and very cold feeling. I turned on the lights, and to my surprise, Linnell was just sitting there looking upset.

I mean, he was really upset, so I asked him why was he sitting in the dark and he said that he was waiting for me to come home. And then he began yelling, saying that I thought he was stupid and that he knew that I was out with someone and I tried to tell him I was at the revival with Ms. Sanita, but he wasn't trying to hear me. He then hauled off and slapped me so hard and I don't know what happened, but I began to fight him back and anything that I could get my hands on I was throwing at him and hitting him with it. He then grabbed me and dragged me to the basement. Once in the basement, we were struggling with his arms around me. Finally, I got away and grabbed the edge clippers for the yard and he came at me and I just stabbed him in the stomach. I wasn't thinking and I could not process what had just happened so I ran back upstairs and called the police.

Once the police arrived, they called the ambulance while the ambulance personnel were attending to Linnell, I told the cops what had happened and they said they will need me to come to the station to press charges, and then they left me there alone. I went back inside and cleaned myself up and I didn't wait till the next day to read those scriptures. I started reading them all night, and to be honest, I read the bible all night until I fell asleep on the couch. The next morning, I got up and read them again, and then went to the station. When I arrived at the station the sergeant met me at the front desk and filled out the paperwork and told me that Linnell was still in the hospital, but when they released him, they were going to pick him up and I would need to show up for court to testify against him.

I could not believe this was happening, I mean I couldn't believe the one person I loved and thought loved me regardless of our kinship, I had to testify against him. After leaving the court I went to Ms. Sanita's to pick up the boys and then went home and just started cleaning and gathering all Linnell's stuff and took it to the trash. You know what was funny is that was the only trash I had to take out. Wow! I guess that's what the pastor meant when he said I was going to clean my house.

February 1999, it was a Monday. I was preparing for court and the phone rang, and when I answered the voice on the other end softly said, "HEY, GIRL! I'm coming to see you, I miss my friend." Yes it was Pat, and Lord, I missed her too. She said I had been on her mind the last couple of nights and she was about to come over. I never knew that Ms. Sanita had called her. She knew everything. She had found out that Linnell was using and was in another relationship. I guess I had a lot of catching up to do. Pat arrived about 8:45 A.M. and we had to be at the court at 9:00 A.M., so as soon as she got there, we left for court. Once we got in the courtroom and were sitting there, they brought Linnell in and he just looked at me with a sadness and I just stared back like this is the day I finally escape the man I loved since childhood, the man

I had given myself to, the man I shared blood with, the forbidden man that had me bound not just as family but as my lover.

Once the judge began speaking, he asked if I wanted to say anything and I told him no. I mean, I just wanted to get out of there. Then the judge started reading all of these other charges that I had no knowledge of and my heart stopped. He then told Linnell that he was going to have to do five years and asked if I will consider moving because he felt as if once Linnell was released. He would come for me. I sadly looked at the judge and said yes, and he said, "Great. Court is adjourned." So Pat and I got up and left and Linnell was led out while yelling he was sorry.

December 24, 1999, I was finally feeling like I was getting my life together. I was working and in school, plus I was reading my bible every day and had begun going to church on a regular basis and began praying every day and having bible study. I had gotten a new car and house and I had met a really great guy, but I had become celibate. Yes, me celibate! Pat and I were hanging out like we used to do, and me, the boys and Pat were getting baptized on Christmas Day. I finally felt like a real person. I didn't have any worries. I felt as if this was the way I was supposed to live this whole time. I didn't have any thoughts of Linnell and he didn't know where I lived and couldn't get to me. Until one night Pat and I went out for dinner with her husband and the guy I had started seeing after arriving back home there was a message on my answering machine from Linnell's mother, she wanted me to call her. I waited till the next day to call and when I called, she answered by asking me a lot of questions about how I was and where I was and that she needed the address to send the boys some things.

I mean, I didn't think nothing of it because we were family and she had no idea what had happened with Linnell and me. She thought that he was locked up for stealing cars and drugs. So, I gave her the address and Pat didn't think I should have done that, so you know by now I had told Pat everything about Linnell and I, I felt like with everything out in the open, she would understand, and she did, but she was against me giving out the address.

January 1, 2000, I thought everything was still going great. We had a nice Christmas. We were baptized and Linnell's mom sent the boys and me a lot of gifts. I was set to graduate in May and I was going to start my new job as a nurse at this private medical center and I was just so happy and then the LETTERS BEGAN!

www.ingramcontent.com/pod-product-compliance
Lightning Source LLC
Chambersburg PA
CBHW050814160726
48004CB00002B/842